CW00969972

THE DINNER LADIES
CLEAN UP

**Also by the same author,
and available in Knight Books:**

THE HEADMASTER WENT SPLAT!
THE SCOURGE OF THE DINNER LADIES
THE CASE OF THE FEEBLE WEEBLE

The Dinner Ladies Clean Up

David Tinkler

Illustrated by David McKee

KNIGHT BOOKS
Hodder and Stoughton

For Christabel Tinkler

Copyright © 1990 by David Tinkler
Illustrations copyright © 1990 by
Anderson Press Limited

First published in Great Britain in 1990
by Anderson Press Limited

Knight edition 1991
Third impression 1991

*The characters and situations in this book are
entirely imaginary and bear no relation to any
real person or actual happenings.*

The right of David Tinkler to be identified as the author of this work and of
David McKee to be identified as the
illustrator of this work has been asserted
by them in accordance with the Copyright, Designs and Patents Act 1988.

This book is sold subject to the condition that it shall not, by way of trade or
otherwise, be lent, re-sold, hired out or
otherwise circulated without the publisher's prior consent in any form of
binding or cover other than that in
which it is published and without a
similar condition including this condition being imposed on the subsequent
purchaser.

No part of this publication may be
reproduced or transmitted in any form
or by any means, electronically or
mechanically, including photocopying,
recording or any information storage or
retrieval system, without either the
prior permission in writing from the
publisher or a licence, permitting
restricted copying. In the United
Kingdom such licences are issued by
the Copyright Licensing Agency,
90 Tottenham Court Road, London
W1P 9HE.

Printed and bound in Great Britain
for Hodder and Stoughton Children's
Books, a division of Hodder and
Stoughton Ltd., Mill Road, Dunton
Green, Sevenoaks, Kent TN13 2YA.
(Editorial Office: 47 Bedford Square,
London WC1B 3DP) by Cox &
Wyman Ltd., Reading.

British Library C.I.P.

Tinkler, David
 The dinner ladies clean up.
 I. Title
 823[J]

 ISBN 0 340 54162 8

Chapter 1

The Third Year Juniors sat still as statues while the little nit nurse moved briskly from head to head. She gripped a magnifying glass in one hand and a nit-flit in the other; a nit-flit is a special flit for swatting nits with. Every so often the still, silent Third Years heard a sinister

SWISH

– as the little nurse pounced. It was difficult not to yelp when that happened to you; swatted children had to grip their tables hard with their hands, grit their teeth and grind them.

'Nits is evil!' croaked the Chief Nurse. She was standing in front of the class. 'They make a lair in your hair! They chews your skin and burrows in!' She chuckled softly – a deep down, hidden sound like boiling mud.

''Ere's a little head what's 'opping wiv 'em!' squawked the little nit nurse eagerly. She was peering through her magnifying glass at a red-headed girl's red hair; the red-headed girl, who was called Caroline Crisp, glanced up and saw the little nurse's horribly huge eye magnified frighteningly like a watching jelly.

'If it's that bad we shall have to shave 'er 'air off of

'er 'ead and burn it,' advised the Chief wisely.

'What, burn 'er 'air or burn 'er 'ead?' asked the little nit nurse.

''Er'air of course. Then, when she's bald we can dip 'er.'

'Dipper?'

'Yeh. Dip her. It's good stuff that dip – pongs a bit – but it does the trick. No nit will come near her!'

'No,' gurgled the little one. 'No more will anything else!'

Caroline went deadly pale when she heard this; it was as if a worried cloud of freckles had settled on a snowball. But she was a fearless girl who had read all the Famous Five books – if the nurses said she had to be dipped, then she would be brave and not cry. She sat looking nervous but noble while the other kids nudged each other and sniggered.

'This way,' croaked the Chief Nurse, 'we've got our special nitmobile parked in the playground – we'll do it out there so this lot don't laugh at you. Don't worry, love, your hair will probably grow again.' Then the two nurses led Caroline out to the playground. The rest of the children waited eagerly for her to come back.

But she did not return!

Chapter 2

Miss Thrasher, the Head Teacher of Littlesprat Primary School, sat in her snug office reading a detective story. Now that thrashing children had been banned, there was not much for her to do, and she spent most of her time reading Miss Marple mysteries.

There was a nervous tap on the door – a knock-knock sort of tap, not a nervous water tap. Understand?

'Come in,' she called. Sherbet Lemon, the Third

Years' teacher, popped into the room. His real name was Herbert Lennon, but the children called him Sherbet Lemon because he was so sweet.

'What's the matter?' frowned the Thrasher.

'I ... I'm worried about the nit nurses ...'

'What nit nurses?'

'The ones that came in through the window ...'

'What!'

'They suddenly climbed in through the window,' explained the worried teacher. 'They said they wanted to take the nits by surprise.'

'But we aren't expecting any nit nurses! Where are they now?'

'That's what I'm worried about. They took Caroline Crisp ...'

'What do you mean?'

'They took her out to their nitmobile – to shave her head and dip her – and they haven't brought her back!'

Miss Thrasher leapt to her feet: what luck! After months of having nothing to do – here was a great mystery to solve.

'Shouldn't we 'phone the police?' asked Sherbet. A shadow passed over the Thrasher's happy face.

'Yes, I suppose we must,' she replied gloomily. 'I really wanted to solve this mystery myself. It would be a good start for my career as an amateur detective and crime-buster. Still, the police round here are so thick they won't be much competition. Is it only

9

Caroline Crisp that's been taken?'

'Yes. Only Caroline.'

'Never mind. One is better than nothing,' smiled the Head. 'I think I'll just take a look at the car park before I ring the police station. There might be some important clues.'

'But shouldn't the police see them first?' protested the Lemon.

'No,' replied Miss Thrasher, 'that would not be fair!'

The two teachers went out to look at the place where the nitmobile had been parked. It was gone, of course, but the nurses had left a clue. Yes: a cheery set of joke shop teeth were lying on the ground.

'Look!' gasped Mr Lennon. 'Those are the teeth the chief nurse had, I thought she looked a bit peculiar!'

Miss Thrasher stooped down, picked them up and put them into her pocket.

'But you shouldn't touch clues!' protested the Lemon.

'Don't be silly, the teeth will come to no harm in my pocket. I really have no confidence at all in the police – they always caused Miss Marple and Sherlock Holmes no end of trouble. I have no intention of giving them the teeth. We found them first after all. Now I'll go and ring them. You, Herbert, had better get back to your class.'

Whenever Third Year Juniors are left by them-

10

selves without a teacher in the class room, they behave in a most studious and dignified manner. Third Year Juniors are never naughty on such occasions; they merely take out their Maths books, without being told, and work at them industriously. Sometimes a Third Year Junior will look up mildly and, in a quiet and serious voice, ask another Third Year Junior for help with a tricky sum. But that is all the noise they make. You can hear the clock tick.

That is why Sherbet Lemon was so shocked to find that there was a riot going on. A girl called Lucasta Smirk was break-dancing and dear little Fatima Zonk was howling tunefully while sweet, young Sharon Slurrey was deftly lashing Fatty Hardcastle's shoelaces together using a knot she'd learnt at Brownies. A boy known as Wayne Drain was competing with Fatima by performing an impression of Miss Thrasher singing in the bath while another boy was lying restfully on the floor wondering whether it was Tuesday. This boy was called Craig Vague; he was always wondering what day it was.

The riot stopped when Mr Lennon came in. All the children turned and gaped eagerly at the opening door; they were hoping to see Caroline with her head shaved and dipped. When they saw dear Sherbet they could not help giving a sigh of disappointment.

'Sir! Sir! Where's Caroline, sir?' cried the keen and

11

eager Third Years.

'She's been kidnapped,' announced Mr Lennon gravely.

'Who kidnapped her, sir?'

'Do they want lots of money, sir?'

'Where have they taken her, sir?'

'Ssh!' shushed Sherbet. 'Sit down and be quiet. The police will be here shortly. I expect they will want to ask you a lot of questions.'

'But sir, that's not fair, sir – suspecting us, sir!'

'We didn't do it, sir!'

'It wasn't us, sir!'

'BE QUIET!' cried Sherbet in his most peeved voice. 'No one suspects you! The police will want to ask you if you've seen anything suspicious.'

The children were silent. Deep thought went on in those Third Year brains. Then *all* those Third Year mouths opened at once and yapping sounds came out of them. It appeared that all the Third Year Juniors had seen *hundreds* of suspicious things.

'Be quiet!' roared Sherbet. 'Save it all for the police. I'm sure what you have to say will be most useful...Ah! Here they are now!'

The door opened and Miss Thrasher ushered in a dapper little detective with twinkling feet. He was a most important man – the Chief of the Metropolitan Police Ballroom Dance Display Unit.

As you know, some policeman have huge, evil-smelling feet, hairy ears, and no sense of rhythm. But

the members of the Metropolitan Police Ballroom Dance Display Unit are all dainty, sweet-scented little coppers who prance about nimbly on neat feet. It is always uplifting to see them twirling their truncheons and bashing baddies in time to music.

The little detective came twinkling into the Third Year classroom; he smelt of talcum powder, Brylcreem, Amplex and aftershave. The only way you could tell he was a detective was by the cunning gleam in his brown eyes.

'These are the Third Year Juniors,' explained Miss Thrasher just in case he thought they were a troupe of highly-trained chimps. 'And this is their teacher, Mr Lennon.'

The detective said nothing. Instead he tap, tap, tapped on the classroom floor with his dainty feet and tap-danced round in a circle.

'I am...er...something of a detective myself,' continued Miss Thrasher. The detective stopped dancing; his pleasant grin disappeared to be replaced by a frown.

'A what?' he cried.

'An amateur detective – like Miss Marple.'

'Oh, you are, are you? One of *them* are you? We've come across *amateur* detectives before, Miss Thrasher. We know *exactly* what they're like!'

'And what are they like, Inspector?'

'Each and every *amateur* detective I have ever met is a waste of space, Miss Thrasher. I will repeat that phrase just in case you were not quick enough to follow my train of thought. A waste of space! You, boy, do you know what I mean by a waste of space?'

'No, sir,' gulped Craig Vague, who'd been pointed at.

'A person, boy, who is a waste of space is worse than useless! All amateur detectives are worse than useless. What are they?'

'Worse than useless, sir.'

'This boy has a keen mind, Miss Thrasher. So,' he continued, 'we have an *amateur* detective on our hands, have we? Well, where is it?'

'Where's what?' replied Miss Thrasher icily.

'The clue.'

'What clue?'

'Amateur detectives always pick up clues; they finger them and mess them up and keep them to themselves! Hand it over!'

Miss Thrasher glared grimly but she handed over the goofy teeth. The sprightly little chap produced a plastic bag, popped them into it, and dropped it into his pocket. He looked long and hard at Miss Thrasher then shook his head sadly.

'An amateur,' he sighed. 'Don't you understand anything about detecting? These teeth have been in someone's mouth, haven't they?'

'Yes – the chief nurse had them in hers,' squeaked Mr Lennon.

'They will most likely have finger prints on them,

and gum prints; we can most likely analyse the spit
and see what she had for breakfast! Amateur detectives! They are useless. And the reason they are
useless is that they are not artful enough. They fail to
understand the first rule of detection: IT IS AL-
WAYS THE LAST PERSON YOU'D EXPECT IT
TO BE.'

Miss Thrasher snorted with rage. 'We amateur
detectives certainly do know that rule,' she cried. 'It
was us amateurs that discovered it.'

'You may be aware of it, Miss Thrasher, but you are all too dim to understand what it means. I will give you a simple example. If someone came up to you and said they'd seen a six-foot tall, dark-haired man robbing a bank – what sort of criminal would you go looking for?'

'That's obvious,' smiled the Head. 'Any student of Agatha Christie's work knows the answer to that. I should go about looking for a fair-haired, female midget!'

'You see,' cried the little detective. 'That is the mistake all amateurs make. The *last person* they would suspect would actually be a six-foot tall, dark-haired man – but they are *too thick* to realise it! We professional detectives *do* realise it – that is the secret of our success.'

'Indeed,' hissed the cold voice of Miss Thrasher, 'and how would you tackle the case of Caroline Crisp?'

'In the same way,' replied the detective tapping his feet knowingly. 'Who was seen carrying out this crime?'

'Two old bats.'

'Exactly. And that's who we will be looking for – a couple of old bats.'

'In that case it's just as well that I will be on the case myself,' cried Miss Thrasher with a frown. 'It is much more likely to turn out to be two small boys!'

Chapter 3

'Sit in that chair.' That is what the Chief Nurse had ordered Caroline to do when they'd first got into the nitmobile. The Third Year girl had sat down nervously; she'd had to think hard about the Famous Five in order to stay calm and brave.

'We'll just strap you in, dear,' cried the merry, little nurse snapping a strap round Caroline's tummy. But instead of shaving the frightened girl's red hair off, the Chief Nurse suddenly chuckled and pulled off her own nurse hat. Caroline gasped when she saw her do that because the nurse hat had been pinned to her hair with hair grips and the hair came off too – it was a wig!

'That's better!' croaked the Chief Nurse scratching her skinhead. It was not until she had taken out her goofy teeth and tossed them out of the window, that Caroline realised who she really was.

'Granny Fang!' she shrieked. Then she went 'MMMM...' because the little nurse had gagged her.

Granny Fang had once been the school cook, but she and the other dinner ladies had really been members of a most desperate gang of crooks – and they had *forced* Caroline to join them. They'd wanted someone young, you see, to do the clambering and climbing for them. Thieves have to clamber and climb a lot, as I expect you realise, and it's hard to do that when you're old and fat.

Yes, Caroline had been a reluctant apprentice thief in the Granny Fang Gang until she'd managed to escape. And now they'd caught her again!

'Remember me, dear?' gurgled the little nurse. She ripped off her hat so Caroline could see who she was. 'That's right, dear, it's me, Batty, what was always so fond of you!'

'I 'spect you're wondrin' where the rest of the gang is, aren't you, dear?' asked Granny Fang. Caroline nodded her head.

'They're in jail,' burbled Batty, 'having a nice rest.'

'Thank goodness,' thought Caroline.

'But don't worry, my love, we're gonna bust 'em out; then we'll all be together again. Won't that be nice?'

Chapter 4

Pay careful attention. Here is a jelly-belly:

WIBBLE

WOBBLE

Imagine a jelly-belly prancing and dancing to disco music. Imagine Granny Fang in a leotard: a most gruesome sight!

'We gotta get fit, Batty,' she panted.

'I am fit,' cackled Batty. This was true: Batty was the only member of the Fang Gang who was skinny.

The thumps and bumps that Granny made as she pranced about echoed shudderingly through to the cellar below. It was usually dark, dank, and restful down there, but with Granny Fang leaping about overhead, it was scary; you never knew when she might crash through the floor and land on your head.

Caroline was sobbing softly down there, you see, locked in the cellar of the Artful Snatcher, the special pub for thieves and muggers. Sometimes she'd feel something ticklish ambling about in her hair – a spider – but she couldn't brush it off because of the way she was chained to the wall. Sometimes she'd hear rats rustling in the darkness, then her flesh would tingle with terror and she'd scream.

Yes, it was horrible chained up in that dark dungeon. No wonder poor little Caroline was crying; no wonder hot tears were oozing out of her green eyes and trickling sadly down her freckled face.

Suddenly a door creaked open high above and a dazzling beam of light shot through the blackness. A voice croaked, 'Well, my pet, have you changed your mind? Are you going to help us? Or do you want to stop down there and starve?'

'I won't help you!' sobbed Caroline bravely. 'I won't go robbing with you and I won't help you bust out Sludge and Slow. They DESERVE to be in jail – AND SO DO YOU!'

'Don't be silly!' cried Batty's little voice. She was standing behind Granny and peering over her shoulder into the damp gloom. 'Thieving's fun – you'll enjoy it.'

'But stealing is bad,' sobbed Caroline. 'I don't want to be bad. I want to be good.'

'You *will* be good, my angel,' Batty reassured her, 'you'll be ever so good at thieving!'

'And you could be famous,' croaked Granny flashing her filed teeth in a friendly smile. 'With your skill and smartness you could be known as the most artful young thief in England!'

But Caroline didn't want to be known as the most artful young thief in England. She wanted to go home and have her tea and sit by the fire reading a Famous Five book.

'I don't want to be a famous thief,' she cried defiantly. 'If I ever become famous I'd like to be famous for being good – like the Famous Five!'

'Who, dear?'

'The Famous Five!'

'What? Muggers are they?'

'No they're not. They're a team of child detectives!'

22

'Detectives are useless!' growled Granny. Then she slammed the door.

'This is your fault, Batty,' croaked the gang leader bitterly as she waddled back into the huge bar and collapsed into a chair. 'It was your idea to kidnap that brat. We'd have done better to have left her alone. If she dies down there and begins to pong we'll get done for murder!'

'She'll change her mind,' chuckled Batty, 'she'll go thieving – don't you worry.'

Usually the bar of the Snatcher was full of muggers and snatchers drinking and fighting happily. But at five o'clock in the afternoon most muggers and snatchers were at home watching 'Grange Hill', so the pair had the place to themselves. But even though they were alone Batty crept up close to Granny and whispered when she explained her plan. As Granny listened her sharkish grin grew wider and her wild eyes gleamed.

Down below in the black cellar, the frightened child listened desperately for noises that could tell her what was going on. Granny seemed to have stopped her disco dancing; there were no thumps or bumps overhead. Once Caroline heard a creak from the ceiling – which was caused by two pairs of feet creeping across the floor above. Once she heard a snort as if someone had been bottling up a snigger. Then the door eased open. This time no light flooded in; instead a gentle whisper came from above.

'I say – you down there – are you all right?'

'No, I'm not,' sniffed Caroline.

'Don't worry,' called a cheerful voice. 'We'll soon have you out!'

'But who are you?' cried the girl.

'We're the FEARLESS FOUR!' was the unexpected answer.

The Fearless Four took a long time to rescue Caroline. This was partly because they didn't want to draw attention to the escape by switching on the light, and partly because Jasper was drunk. He was the one that kept striking matches then swearing and dropping them when they burnt his fingers.

'But there's only two of you!' hissed Caroline when Jasper struck his first match.

'Yes, just Jasper and me – I'm Nick,' explained Nick cheerfully. 'The others have been captured by Granny Fang and we're going to rescue them next.'

The two brave lads loped down the stairs grinning beerily. You may be wondering what grinning *beerily* means – well, it's how you grin if you look eerie to start with and then drink lots of beer.

Caroline was amazed by their huge beards – not that she ever got to look at them very long, particularly after Jasper dropped the matches.

'Are you in the middle of an adventure?' asked the captured girl keenly.

'Yes,' replied a husky voice in the dark. There was a yelp and a tumbling clatter as the fearless rescuers fell down the last few steps and eventually Caroline felt firm hands grip her wrists and heard a scratching at the handcuffs.

'Have you got the key?' she asked excitedly.

'Yes,' grunted Jasper with his beery breath.

'But how did you get it? Granny Fang had it stuffed down the front of her nurse dress.'

'She took it off to go disco dancing and we sort of borrowed it!' laughed Nick cheerily.

'But who are the Fearless Four?' asked Caroline when they'd released her. She was standing in the dark rubbing her wrists because of pins and needles.

'We're like the Famous Five,' hissed Jasper, 'only there's not so many of us.'

'And we're not so famous,' laughed Nick, 'but we're smarter – and better looking!'

'Are those real beards?' asked the wondering child.

'No – of course not,' explained Nick. 'These are special disguises. We don't want to be recognised – especially not here at the Artful Snatcher which is full of the most fearful cut-throats and yobs, as you know. We've got one for you . . .'

'What a yob?'

'No, a beard. Quick put it on – we have a job to do!'

An evil-smelling river wound its slimy way past the Artful Snatcher; often frolicking skinheads threw other skinheads into it, but tonight was 'Crimewatch' night, so all was still. This was just as well for, as darkness fell, three mysterious, bearded figures (one of them quite small) crept out of the pub, climbed down some steps, and scrambled into a little boat that was moored there. Jasper yanked at the outboard motor which sprang to life with a roar.

'You're supposed to untie the boat first!' grinned Nick. While Jasper muttered and wrestled with the rope, Nick eased his rucksack off and fished eagerly inside it. Of all the fearless members of the Fearless Four he was the most dare-devil and carefree. 'I say – ham sandwiches and ginger beer!' he chuckled. 'And, gosh! We are in luck! A nice big bottle of gin!'

What fun it was and how exciting sailing down the dark river with Nick and Jasper. Caroline munched a ham sandwich hungrily; this was a real adventure and she would need all her strength.

'Rest while you can,' Nick advised her kindly. 'We'll soon be rescuing the others and then there'll be plenty of excitement I can tell you!'

Chapter 5

Have you ever been to prison?

I see.

Well, if you ever go into the burgling trade, then I expect you'll spend a few years in jail and find out all about it for yourself. Meanwhile you should know that the worst thing about prisons is the smell. They smell of stink-pots, carbolic soap, festering feet, vomit and armpits. This is why many experienced criminals take little bunches of dried lavender to sniff at when they go to jail. The other prisoners laugh at them, but it is worth it.

The sounds you hear in prison are clanks and clinks and rattles as keys turn in locks; dull, echoing thuds as heavy doors slam shut; howls, growls and sickening thumps. That was what it was like in the New Model Prison: GRIM.

Do you remember what Granny Fang had said had happened to Mrs Sludge and Mrs Slow – the other two members of the Dinner Lady Gang? Well, the New Model Prison was where they were.

Just as Jasper, Nick and Caroline sailed into the tunnel, Mrs Sludge started to trudge down a prison corridor to the longest loo in the world while warders yelped and barked at her.

'Every night it's the same!' muttered the Sludge,

traipsing wearily.

'Shurrup!' screamed a warder. Mrs Sludge took no notice; she went on mumbling and grumbling to Mrs Slow.

'They march us here; they march us there; they blow their wretched whistles at us. What do they think we are? Majorettes?'

'Shurrup!'

At the New Model Prison, the loos had been built over an underground river to save on plumbing. There were fifty cubicles in a row so the prisoners could be marched there fifty at a time just before they went to bed. The warders had just knocked out fifty holes with a drill and made the seats out of old car tyres filled with cement. It was not very comfy – but the New Model Prison did not believe in making its prisoners comfortable. It believed in serving them right. And it believed in a strict routine; every night, *at exactly the same time,* the prisoners were marched to the loos above the underground river.

Mrs Slow sat down on a hard car tyre seat and began to read a horror comic.

'This is a good one!' she yelled.

'Shurrup!'

'What is?' asked Sludge's voice from the next-door cubicle.

'This comic Batty sent us. It's about this castle what's haunted!'

'Shurrup!'

'Haunted?'

'Yeh, haunted. There's vampires and ghosts of evil people what have died there and they go about haunting and...'

'Shurrup!'

Slow turned the page. She didn't actually read much but she liked looking at the pictures of the monsters and spooks. She liked stuff like that...

She was just looking at a picture of someone going Ahhh! with their hair standing on end when she heard a real scream.

One of the prisoners had howled.

Then: EEEK! She heard a startled EEK.

Then: YELP! Somebody yelped.

'Shurrup!'

Mrs Slow stopped looking at her comic. What was happening? People kept going OW! and OO! It was frightening.

Yes – frightening. That is what young Caroline thought as she sat in the front of the boat holding high the flaming torch so that it flickered against the arched ceiling.

Above, in the prison, Mrs Slow sat on the old tyre with her ears practically flapping as she listened to the yelps and cries of the other prisoners. First one would squeak, and then the next. What could be happening? Then she jumped; something hot had stung her. A flickering flame had shot up from the underground river. Mrs Slow screamed.

'Shurrup!' roared the warder.

'Is it ghosts?' asked Caroline below.

'Ssh!' hissed Nick. 'This is the place. I recognised that last yell. Unless I'm very much mistaken that was *Gwendoline* sitting up there. And that means *Horace* will be up the next hole!'

'But I thought the others in the Fearless Four were both girls,' cried Caroline.

'They are,' whispered Nick. 'Horace is just a nickname. Her real name is Doris only she insists on being called Horace instead.'

'Just like George in the Famous Five,' laughed

Caroline eagerly. Little tingles of excitement were oozing round her tummy. What fun this was!

'Yes,' nodded Nick grinning in the torch light, 'the Famous Five copy a lot of what we do.'

While Caroline and Nick had been whispering, Jasper had dropped anchor.

'All right, Caroline, this is where we rescue the others,' he whispered. 'All you have to do is climb up that hole in the roof.'

Caroline glanced upwards; there seemed to be a series of holes drilled into the tunnel roof.

'Shouldn't we call out to them if they're up there,' asked the eager girl.

'We can't shout,' replied Nick, 'or the ward... or *Granny Fang* might hear us. But you being so small and me being middle-sized and Jasper being big – we can form a human pyramid like in a circus and you can poke this up the hole for Horace.'

'What is it?'

'A sledgehammer. All she has to do is belt at the hole until it's big enough for her and Gwendoline to climb through. Then they'll land in the river – we'll fish 'em out and sail for home!'

'Brilliant!'

'Well,' whispered Nick modestly, 'it was Jasper's idea not mine. And a jolly good one too!'

It was frightening clambering onto Nick's shoulders. The boat rocked dangerously even though Jasper had jammed it sideways across the width of the tunnel to make it stable. The hole was slobbery and cold. It stank and its sides were coated in gunge and slime. But when you are helping adventurers like the Fearless Four, you don't worry so much about things like that. You just get on with it in a brave and cheerful manner.

'Here's the hammer,' hissed Jasper.

Caroline lugged the heavy sledgehammer up towards the slime-hole.

'Here goes!' she hissed and thrust the handle upward into the inky, stinky darkness.

It hit something soft. There was an enraged roar of pain; hands seized the handle and the hammer was torn from her grasp.

'Quick,' yelped Nick. 'Get down! We've got to get the boat clear before she starts. She'll be fast, mind. She's got to be!'

They scrambled back; Jasper hauled up the anchor, and the little boat shot back down the tunnel just as the first hammer blows fell on the bricks above. Soon rubble was raining down into the water.

'It's a good thing we're not underneath now,' squeaked Caroline.

'That's nothing!' croaked Jasper. 'Just wait till they jump. Then there'll be a splash and a half!'

Above them Mrs Sludge was attacking the floor of the cubicle; she'd knocked down the partition between Slow and herself and they were both eager

to escape.

'Ready, Slow! Don't worry about the warden – I'll take care of her. The hole's big enough! Jump!'

Below the little boat bobbed crazily as Jasper moved suddenly towards the bow. 'You done very well,' he hissed to Caroline. 'Now be a brave girl and hop into this sack!'

'Why?' cried the eager child.

'It's a disguise,' explained Nick urgently. 'Something we often do on adventures when there's a danger of being captured. One of us hides in a sack – then, if the others get caught, there's always someone left to do something about it. You'll look like a sack of stores, you see, and just be left behind.'

Gosh! What a brilliant scheme! Caroline hopped into the sack and felt Jasper tie it up with strong cord. It was dark and smelt deeply sack-like; the boat continued bobbing and then – SPLASH! SPLASH! – it bucked about. More splashing; voices; the little boat heeled over – Gwendoline and Horace were being hauled aboard.

'Ssh!' Jasper greeted them. 'Don't say anything!' Then the engines roared and the boat surged forward.

What an adventure! The engine's roar echoing in the tunnel; the hard, bucking floor; the coarse sack – Caroline couldn't help hoping that Granny Fang was chasing them in a speed boat. Yes. She almost wished Granny Fang would catch the others so she could rescue them all by herself.

She kept mouse quiet and statue still trying madly to imagine that she was a sack of food. 'I'll pretend to be a huge bag of crisps,' she chuckled to herself, 'because I'm called Caroline Crisp!'

The escape went on for ages. At one point they left the boat and, to judge from the lurching, swinging and bumping, Caroline's sack was carried along over Jasper's shoulder for a while. Then she was plonked gently onto the ground. Nick's voice hissed in her ear, 'Just stay still a minute.'

Eventually she felt hands tugging at the knot and her head popped out of the sack.

'Is everything okay?' she whispered.

'Yes,' grinned Nick. Caroline looked about; she was sitting in long grass; stars twinkled above; she could see huge clumps of nettles and old lager cans glinting in the moonlight.

'It's a secret garden known only to us,' explained Nick in a low voice. 'It used to be a beer garden – of a pub, you understand – only the landlord was so lazy he fenced it off. Now it's like a little private park. We'll be safe here so don't worry; I've got you a tent and a sleeping-bag. I suggest you turn in and get some kip. It's very late for a little one – and remember we're still in the middle of an adventure: tonight was just the start. You'll need all your strength in the morning – when the action really starts!'

Chapter 6

'S'all right!' gurgled Batty tearing off her beard and collapsing into a chair. 'The poor little sap's fast asleep – bless her little cotton socks.'

'I 'spect the fresh air has tired 'er,' croaked Granny.

'Yeh. It was certainly fresh up that hole,' laughed Batty. 'Tire anyone that would!'

The two thieves sat at the bar of the Artful Snatcher and shook with laughter until Slow and Sludge joined them. They'd been upstairs changing out of their wet prison clothes into their Gwendoline and Horace outfits. Slow didn't see the point of her new disguise. 'What I got to wear this for?' she grumbled. 'I looks like I've fallen out of a Christmas tree!'

'Ssh!' croaked Granny. 'Batty's gotta plan. A real good 'un!'

'Has she?' grunted Sludge. 'Well I hope it's better than the last plan you had – that's all!' She glared at Granny like a wild beast that was hungry. 'Whose idea was it to make that mad kid stick that stick up that hole? Why couldn't you of busted us out with a helicopter same as last time?'

'That's gratitude for you!' shrieked Granny. 'We bust you out and we've gotta plan all ready to make you rich and all we get is grumbles. Next time you're nicked we'll leave you in there to rot!'

'I left my comic in the jail,' sighed Slow.

'Well,' replied Granny, 'we are not going back for it!'

'Can I go there tomorrow and knock on the door and ask for it?' asked Slow hopefully.

'No you can't. You gotta change, Slow. You can't go about reading horror comics no more. You gotta remember to be Gwendolin'. Gwendolin' wouldn't read horror comics.'

'Who's Gwendolin'?'

'You are,' explained Batty seriously. 'You are

GWEN-DO-LIN' – that's who you are now – okay?'

'Yur.'

'Say it then – say your name.'

'Your – name.'

'No. Say your new name – Gwendolin'!'

'Your new name – Gwendolin'.'

'That's close. Now listen. You are now Gwendolin' not Slow. Understand? You ain't Slow no more...'

'What? You mean I'm quick?'

'No. You're still slow meaning thick but your name ain't Slow no more, is it?'

'No.'

'So, what's your new name?'

There was a puzzled silence.

'It starts with G,' croaked Granny helpfully. Slow thought slowly about things that started with G. This was hard. She had a feeling that cheese began with G but didn't say anything.

'Gwendolin',' explained Batty wearily. 'You are now called Gwendolin' and you are a member of the Fearless Four. And Granny ain't Granny no more she's Jasper.'

Slow blinked wisely.

'She's a boy, okay? Called Jasper,' continued Batty earnestly. 'He's a big-headed sort of bloke wot keeps telling everyone what to do...'

'Same as when she was Granny?'

'That's right. Jasper is the leader and I'm Nick –

who is also a boy only more cheerful and carefree. I says things like, "I say, what jolly fun!" and stuff like that, see? In a posh voice, understand?'

'Yer.'

'You've gotta talk posh too. You've gotta say things like, "Oh I hate spiders!" see? All posh. Can you do that?'

'Yer.'

'Go on then, say it – posh, mind.'

'Oh I 'ate spiders!'

'No, Gwendolin', you never ate no spiders you hate 'em too much!' squawked Batty.

'Oh.'

'You'd better keep your mouth shut as much as you can. But don't worry. The girl's so green she won't catch on. Now, Gwendolin', listen carefully. I've not finished yet. Sludge is now Horace. But it ain't her real name; her real name is Doris.'

'But her real name is Sludge!'

'I know. But her real pretend name is Doris only she don't like being called Doris so she calls herself Horace. See?'

There was another silence. This one was even more puzzled than the one before.

'Just get it into your thick skull,' growled Granny. 'We are now the Fearless Four – two boys and two girls – and you is the one what is always frightened and screaming and trembling in a girly way, see? And Sludge is the other girl what is always playing

41

football and fighting – like a boy, see?'

'Ain't we a bit big for boys and girls?'

'We're big boys and girls. We eats our greens up, don't we? So who are you, Slow?'

Slow grinned triumphantly. 'Cheese!' she cried.

Chapter 7

Caroline awoke to hear the clank of pans and the sizzle of frying bacon. From somewhere near, Nick's cheerful voice called out, 'Gosh, Gwendoline, what a ripping smell! There's nothing like living under canvas to work up an appetite. Am I the last to wake up?'

'No – you – ain't,' answered a slow voice.

That must have been one of the girls that had been rescued the night before. Caroline couldn't wait to meet them; she leapt out of her snug sleeping-bag – which is usually hard to do because sleeping-bags are warm and cosy while tents are damp and clammy. Her bare feet could feel the cold earth under the ground-sheet as she padded about hunting for her beard, and her deeply freckled nose could smell the tent and squashed grass scent you get when you're camping. The beard was dank and clammy damp, but she put it on all the same because Nick had warned her about the terrible risk of being caught again. 'I'm sure we're quite safe camping here, but you must never under-estimate Granny Fang; her spies are everywhere,' he had told Caroline solemnly. 'We must wear our beards all the time, and you, Caroline, must wear these special dark specs because you are the one most at risk. Here are a pair of jeans and jumper. We will burn your school uniform on the camp-fire.'

Caroline didn't mind the beard, even though it itched and got in the way when she was eating, but she hated the dark glasses; she could hardly see a thing when she had them on – they were so black. But despite this discomfort, it was wonderful being on an adventure with the Fearless Four – and now she was going to meet the two girls. What would Horace be like? Moody? Cross? But Gwendoline was sure to be sweet and kind! With a tingle in her tum, the freckled child pushed open her tent flap and scrambled into the sunlight to meet her new friends.

The thistles were still wet with dew, wood smoke hung amongst the nettles; Nick and Jasper were standing near their tents talking earnestly together, while crouching over the camp-fire clutching a billy-can was a big, tall, plump, pig-tailed girl in a pink Laura Ashley party frock with matching beard. Huge hair-grips, like plastic butterflies, stuck out behind her ears.

'You must be Gwendoline,' Caroline greeted her.

'Yes I must,' agreed the strange girl. 'I have got to be Gwendoline. That is who I am. Gwendolin'. It starts with G.'

'I'm Caroline,' laughed Caroline. 'I start with C.'

'No,' replied the girl solemnly. 'You start with bacon.' She thrust a bacon sandwich into Caroline's hand. It was hot and smoky. Fat oozed down her fingers. Caroline took a bite and looked about for the second girl. One of the tents trembled and an angry head with plaits popped out.

'Oh, here is Horace,' cried Gwendoline. ''Er real name is Doris,' she continued in a loud whisper, 'but if you call her Doris she don't like it. Look – I'll show you. 'ULLO DORIS!'

'Don't call me Doris!' screamed Horace. 'You know I *hate* it! I can't think why Mama and Papa could ever think of calling me such a *beastly* name!'

'I 'spect they looked at you and said, "Don't she look a beastly baby, let's call 'er somethink beastly," ' explained Gwendoline.

'You cow, Gwendolin'! What a really horrid thing to say!' screamed Horace red with rage.

'I think Gwendoline was only making a little joke,' explained Caroline. 'I'm sure she didn't mean to offend you.'

Horace wheeled round and glared at the child. 'Who – or what – are you?' she snarled.

'She's the little kid what poked the stick up the hole,' explained Gwendoline.

'Oh, she is is she?' hissed Horace. 'Well I don't see why we've got to put up with her! It's always best when it's just the four of us having adventures on our own! But Nick's so daft he's always inviting along complete Wallies to muck things up. Monkeys and dwarfs and SILLY LITTLE GIRLS with freckles!'

45

Horace's head disappeared into her tent again.

'She's gonna sulk now,' explained Gwendoline. 'She'll most probably sit in her tent all day refusing to talk to anyone till Nick goes in and tells her to buck up and be a brick – or Jasper goes in and tells her to buck up or he'll hit her with one.'

Somehow Caroline had known that Horace would be like this. Difficult.

'She always was a pain,' explained Gwendoline slowly, 'but she has got worse since...' She was going to say, *since she started pretending to be Horace,* but stopped herself just in time.

'Hi there, Caro,' called a cheery voice. Nick and Jasper had finished their serious talk and had come over to the camp-fire. 'Any chance of another mug of coffee, Gwendoline?' he asked hopefully.

'Why don't you make it yourself,' she replied. 'Why do I have to do all the cooking?'

'Because you *like* cooking, Gwendoline, remember?' growled Jasper.

'Yes, yes! Oh, I am frightened of the dark! Help! Help! I hate spiders!'

'But it's not dark,' grinned Nick.

'And there aren't any spiders that I can see,' laughed Caroline. Everyone chortled with laughter. Even the sulking tent stopped sulking and rocked instead.

Yes – it was a happy-go-lucky team of crime-busters that young Caroline had met up with. Jasper

was the oldest member of the Four, a bulky, bald-headed boy with an extra-bushy beard. Nick and Horace were next; Horace looked more like a wilde-beest than a girl and, as you've seen, she went into the most ferocious strops if people called her Doris instead of Horace. Gwendoline was the youngest, the one that loved cooking and washing-up; everyone laughed like mad whenever she cracked one of her odd little jokes.

What fun this was, thought Caroline, and how ripping it would be if they asked her to join them – to be a full-time member – they'd be called the FEAR-LESS FIVE. That's what Caroline secretly hoped, you see. She kept thinking that if she did really, really well at mystery-solving and stayed brave and didn't cry, they might ask her. That would be wonderful; it made her green eyes gleam behind her dark glasses just to think about it.

'I say, Caroline,' said Nick, 'you were frightfully brave for a young 'un yesterday and Jasper and I have been talking about how smart and keen you are...'

'Yes!'

'...And we were wondering if you'd like to help us get the better of Granny Fang and her gang...'

'What do you want me to do?' asked the delighted child.

'Well, it's a question of helping us get back all the stuff that Granny Fang has stolen...'

'What?'

'Yes. You see she has bribed all sorts of important people to mind her loot – bank managers and people like that – Jasper has a list of them and what we plan to do is raid them one by one and steal it back. Then we can return it all to the poor people the gang stole it from.'

'But,' gasped Caroline, 'wouldn't it be easier just to give the list to the police?'

Nick shook his head sadly. 'That's what we would have done in a normal adventure,' he sighed, 'but there's nothing normal about the Fang Gang. Granny Fang and Batty are the most cunning villains we have ever come up against. And what makes them especially hard to catch is the way they bribe important people to help them by giving them money – often the very people who ought, by rights, to be out looking for them...'

'You mean they've bribed the police?' cried Caroline amazed.

'Exactly. At least we're absolutely sure that they have bribed the Metropolitan Police Dance Display Unit...'

'But that's awful!'

'Yes,' croaked Jasper. He nodded his head in agreement and frowned seriously. 'There's far too much of that sort of thing going on nowadays!' he said sadly.

Nick waited a moment to make sure the leader

didn't want to say anything else about the disgraceful conduct of the Dance Display Unit, then he continued: 'We have reason to believe that the Display Unit are guarding a vast hoard of stolen treasure for the Fang Gang. This is why we need your help, Caroline. We've got a plan to get it back...'

'But how?'

'Well, it will be a very dangerous operation. Are you brave enough to give it a go?'

'Yes!' said Caroline firmly.

Here was her big chance!

Chapter 8

'Good afternoon,' said Miss Thrasher, 'what did you want to see me about?'

'I have been giving powerful thought to the Caroline Crisp case and, as a result of our inquiries, we are able to rule out kidnapping for a ransom,' replied the dapper detective.

'How have you been able to do that?'

'Simple. No ransom has been asked for.'

'I see. And is that as far as you've got?'

'Certainly not. I have drawn up a plan for a house to house search of the neighbourhood which will start next week.'

'Why not start immediately?'

'I would like to have been able to start immediately, but unfortunately my Display Team are practising hard for the semi-finals of the British Isles Tango Competition. It's on Saturday night so we will start the search on Monday.'

'But surely they should be out catching criminals and searching for Caroline now – not dancing about all day!'

'They are quite often out catching criminals,' replied the detective crossly. 'They catch them on Mondays and Fridays – it's only on Tuesdays, Wednesdays, Thursdays, Saturdays and Sundays that they have a chance to practise their dance routines. We are a champion team, you know. You should see the cups we've won – gold ones, silver, a cup encrusted with diamonds and rubies given us by the King of Spain after we'd won the Eurovision Truncheon Twirling Contest. Our trophies are so valuable we have to keep them locked in a strong-room guarded night and day by a squad of disco-dancing martial arts constables.'

'Humph!' humphed Miss Thrasher scornfully. 'No wonder there are so many thieves and muggers about!'

'Not at all. The attention we give to dancing makes us better at catching thieves and muggers. We are nimbler on our feet, you see, because of the dancing. And our minds are keen. Also we only drink fizzy drinks, whereas ordinary policemen constantly swill beer which slows them down considerably. Anyway, come and see the trophies; they'll take your breath away! Follow me, the strong-room is off the ballroom.'

A spruce team of police guards snapped to attention as the detective and Miss Thrasher approached the strong-room door. (A strong-room is a room that is strong – okay? It's like a huge safe the size of a room.)

'Miss Thrasher, I must ask you to turn away while I twiddle the combination lock,' requested the dapper detective. 'We can take no chances with valuable police property.'

Miss Thrasher turned her back while the little chap grunted and heaved at the huge door until it swung slowly open. 'You may turn round,' he told her.

Beyond the open door lay a small, windowless room with a purple carpet and rows of empty shelves. The little detective gaped, gasped, then folded up like a deck-chair. He had fainted. He lay in a heap on the purple carpet. The disco-dancing guards crowded round anxiously.

'The trophies are gone!' one of them gulped.

'But how? We've been here all the time!'

'Yes – and the walls are eight foot thick!'

Miss Thrasher, the amateur detective, could not help grinning a sweet little grin as she watched the confusion. One of the guards pressed an alarm bell and soon troupes of dancing police tripped anxiously into the ballroom. They chattered and buzzed excitedly until one of the guards called out, 'The Chief's out cold. Has anyone any suggestions?'

'I suggest we calm ourselves with a slow foxtrot,' cried an earnest young copper earnestly.

'No, that's stupid!' cried a policewoman. 'We should cheer ourselves up with some break-dancing!'

The dancing cops didn't stop arguing about what sort of dance to do until a team of cleaning ladies lumbered into the strong-room chattering and clat-

tering their mops and buckets.

'You're not supposed to be here,' croaked one of them.

'This is our time to polish the ballroom floor. It's got to be done properly if you want to glide and slide.'

This was true; the police team knew that the ballroom floor had to be treated very carefully; but this was a crisis.

'Go away!' shrieked one of them. 'A terrible crime has been committed; we need to dance: You can do the floor another day.'

'But it's our job to do it now. We polish the ballroom floor and hoover the strong-room carpet.'

'That's true,' agreed one of the disco-dancers. 'We guard them while they do it.'

'So what?' cried a fragrant policewoman.

'Get them out of here!' agreed a stately sergeant. 'Them and all their stuff.' He glared angrily at the buckets.

Muttering and grumbling the cleaning ladies clattered out of the strong-room heaving a vast vacuum cleaner behind them.

'Come on, girls,' snapped their leader. 'I'm not stopping where we're not wanted!'

As the ladies waddled away, a murmur arose from the policewomen that were looking after the Chief. Miss Thrasher glanced into the strong-room and saw that he had come round. They were helping him to his feet.

'We have been wondering what to do, sir,' a guard told him quietly.

'I should have thought that was obvious,' snorted the little chap. 'In a case like this, there's only one thing to do – call the police!'

Chapter 9

'The police are totally feeble,' declared Miss Thrasher triumphantly. 'They can't even guard their own valuables. It is only amateur detectives like Miss Marple and myself that have any idea of how to outwit the criminal mind.'

'Oh,' replied Sherbet Lemon doubtfully. So far he had not seen Miss Thrasher outwit any criminals.

'What do you mean, "Oh"? Only last week I invented a revolutionary new crime-busting device,' claimed Miss Thrasher modestly. 'It's TOP SECRET – the police must not find out or they'll start using them too.'

The two teachers were sitting in Miss Thrasher's office counting dinner money. Dinner money is difficult to count because of the way children tend to bring the wrong amounts; that is why it usually takes two people to work it out.

'Well, I won't tell anyone,' said the Lemon.

'Perhaps later – when I'm famous – you could tell the world about my invention,' answered Miss Thrasher. 'In fact you could write books about me like Dr Watson did for Sherlock Holmes. One of the books could be called after my invention; it would make a snappy book title: *The Pants of Power!*'

'Pants of power?'

'Precisely. The pants, Herbert, of power.'

'But what are they?'

Miss Thrasher glanced sharply out of the window in case anything evil like a criminal or a policeman or a child was watching, then she stood up and sauntered about the floor. She looked like a cross between a fashion model on 'The Clothes Show' and a clown in a circus. 'You may have noticed,' she whispered, 'that I am wearing a natty pair of pantaloons.'

'Everyone has noticed that,' blurted the Lemon. 'The children have made up a song about them...'

'I am not interested in the tuneless warbling of juveniles; these pantaloons may look to you like a fashionable pair of culottes – the sort of thing you might see a model wearing.'

'The children seem to think that they are the sort of thing a fashionable bag-woman might wear...'

'Well, they might look a bit baggy and saggy, but no one would ever guess what they really were. Look – see these rip cords?'

'Rip cords?'

'Yes. These little bits of string dangling down.'

'Yes. They are mentioned in the children's song...'

'In an emergency I only have to give them a yank and...I'll show you: menace me as if you were a mugger.'

'What?'

'Pretend to be a baddie. Attack me and see what

happens. Go on!' The mild and kindly Lemon gave a growl like a kitten purring and raised his fist as if he was going to bop the Thrasher on the end of her sharp nose. She grinned, reached down, and pulled one of the rip cords:

WHOOSH!

With a swooshing whoosh, Miss Thrasher's natty pantaloons inflated like a pair of huge rubber dinghies and shot up into the air until they hit the ceiling so that she dangled down like someone hanging by her legs from a trapeze.

'You see,' she cried with her upside-down mouth. 'I've got little gas canisters round my waist and when I pull one of the rip cords, the pants of power inflate like a helium balloon – except much bigger.'

'But what's the point of that?'

'Can't you see? These pants will save me from danger...Say I had tracked down a dangerous murderer and he suddenly sprang at me with a knife – then WHOOSH – I'd yank one of the cords and shoot up into the air. See?'

'But what if you were inside a house?'

'Simple. I'd leap out of the window and then – WHOOSH – I'd yank one of the cords and – WHOOSH – instead of crashing to the ground, I'd waft away on the breeze. Now help me down. No – don't pull that rip cord...'

WHOOSH!

The pantaloons doubled in size pressing the luckless Sherbet into the carpet. He lay on the floor listening to Miss Thrasher's cross voice comparing his brain to that of a widgeon. Or was it a pigeon? Her voice was deeply muffled. There was a lot of threshing about up there. 'Shut your eyes,' she suddenly snapped. 'I have managed to loosen the belt and I'm going to wriggle out of the pants.'

'But, Miss Thrasher, you can't go about the school in your knickers. The children would make up another of their songs.'

'Of course I won't go about school. I am a headteacher; I shall simply sit behind my desk reading my Miss Marple book. The pantaloons will slowly shrivel until they are back to normal.'

There were wriggling, slithering sounds followed by a bump. Then Miss Thrasher's cool voice ordered the Lemon to open his eyes. 'Let us get on with our work,' she said as she sat modestly behind her desk.

'Where's the money?' gasped Sherbet.

'It was on the desk.'

'But...'

'Who could possibly have stolen it? We've been here all the time!'

Chapter 10

What fun it was helping the Fearless Four track down the Fang Gang's loot and nicking it back from the baddies that were minding it. Baddies like the Metropolitan Police Ballroom Dance Display Unit and Miss Thrasher. Fancy people like that being in the pay of Granny Fang!

Caroline was doing so well nicking back loot that she had high hopes of being made a full member of the team. 'I'd be like Timmy the Dog!' she told herself eagerly, 'the fifth one of the Fearless Five!' Every time she thought that, her green eyes glistened behind her dark glasses; if Caroline had had a tail she would have wagged it.

'I say, Caroline, you've done awfully well and we're all terribly grateful,' said Nick one night beside the camp-fire. The two of them were toasting marshmallows on sticks.

'I just do what you lot tell me,' replied the modest child. 'You're the ones with all the experience – the ones that have had dozens of adventures already.'

'Yes, but you really are a plucky kid,' said Nick kindly. Caroline wondered if he was about to invite her to join, but, of course, Jasper was the leader of the Fearless Four; he would be the one to invite her, but Caroline could tell that Nick was secretly busy persuading the others that she was a good enough crimebuster to join the team as a full member. All she had to do was keep being keen and brave.

There was a noise like a frog barking – one of Jasper's burps. He joined them round the fire and began whispering in Nick's ear. As he listened a look of outrage spread over Nick's face. Jasper had some photographs in his hand; Nick took one and stared at it hard shaking his head and frowning. This must be really serious, thought the watching girl.

'Caroline,' said Nick eventually, turning urgently towards her. 'Jasper has some grave news.'

'Grave?' cried the worried child. 'Has somebody died?'

'Not yet,' croaked Jasper darkly. Caroline had never seen him so upset.

'Look at this photograph,' said Nick, taking one of the snaps and showing it to her.

'It's the Queen!'

'Exactly. Now look at this one.'

'It's another photograph of the Queen.'

'Is it? Examine it carefully. Compare it with the first.'

Caroline studied the two photographs intently in the firelight. They looked exactly the same to her but she didn't want to appear unobservant. Not when they were thinking of making her a full-time member.

'Can you see the difference?'

'Er. Yes. This one seems to be...er...sort of dif-

63

ferent,' said Caroline eventually.

'That's what Jasper thinks, and I must say I agree with him,' replied Nick in a low voice. 'We haven't shown them to the others yet. Jasper wanted you to see them first since you're such a smart kid.' Caroline went pink.

'We wanted to see if you could spot something wrong too,' explained Nick, still speaking in his serious voice. 'If all three of us think the same way about that photograph, then there is almost certainly something going on that we should look into.'

'What do you mean?'

'Well, don't tell the others yet, but Jasper and I think that this picture is not really of the Queen at all. Unless we are very much mistaken that is Batty – the most cunning of the Dinner Ladies. The one that is a master of disguise!'

'What?'

'Yes – Batty must be going about opening Parliaments and launching ships and scoffing banquets and stuff like that...'

'But why?'

'It's obvious. Granny Fang is trying for the big one, the crime of the century...'

'What?' cried Caroline in dismay. 'Not...not the Crown Jewels!'

'I fear so,' Nick answered desperately. Caroline had never seen him like this before; he seemed utterly zapped.

'Couldn't we ring the police or tell the Prime Minister?'

'They wouldn't believe us,' croaked Jasper sadly. 'People would just think we were mad.'

It was then that Caroline had her brilliant plan – the first plan that she ever suggested to the Fearless Four. It just came to her like magic and, before she knew it, she heard her own eager voice blurting keenly. 'I know!' she gasped. 'We can get in first.'

'What do you mean?'

'We can steal them before they do!'

'Brilliant,' cried Nick gazing in frank admiration at the child.

'I think you've got it,' croaked Jasper with a grin. 'I really think you've got the answer! Gosh, how I wish I'd thought of that! But how exactly do we nick 'em? They are guarded night and day in the Tower of London!'

'I know,' replied Caroline nodding her red head. 'But I think there's a way we can do it!'

Chapter 11

As you know, the Tower of London is an enormous castle where people go to get their heads chopped off. It is guarded by trusty Beefeaters armed with keen axes. These Beefeaters are soldiers who are dressed cunningly in uniforms designed to make their enemies curl up with helpless laughter; they wear party hats, pretty ruffs, tights and pantaloons – this is what makes them so terrible in battle. Imagine being leapt at by men in tights and party hats; of course you crease up with laughter, then slish, slash – they whittle you!

The main duty of these cunning soldiers, apart from chewing beef and swigging ale, is to guard the Queen's treasure. Many bold and artful crooks have tried to steal it, but so far none of them has ever succeeded because of these brave men and the highly trained flock of deadly ravens that assists them. Normally the Jewels are kept behind bullet-proof glass, but the alarm system was being renewed, so the glass had been taken out and, every day, a squad of Beefeaters bristling with fearsome axes stood in a grim circle around the tower in which the Jewels were kept. Inside another squad stood round the treasure itself.

At four o'clock on the afternoon following

Caroline's announcement that she had a PLAN, the
door to the treasure tower creaked open and four
cleaning ladies waddled in yapping.

'Is this the treasure stronghold?' asked the leading crone.

The Beefeater in charge calmly swallowed a mouthful of beef and answered her. 'What do you think that is?' he said pointing his axe at the treasure. 'A pile of Smarties? Of course this is the stronghold; these are the Crown jewels and we're here guarding 'em, aren't we? We're not just standing round for the good of our health!'

'All right, all right, keep your hair on,' grumbled the lady, 'and shift yourself; we've gotta hoover round and dust.'

'What do you mean *shift yourself*? You can't tell one of the Queen's Beefeaters to shift himself... not when he's on guard!'

'Oh,' cried a merry little cleaning lady bustling in amongst them, 'now you've hurt his feelings. Don't he look proud though in his fancy dress!'

'No,' growled a third cleaner, a fat-bottomed one with a face like an ironing board. 'He don't look proud in it, he looks stupid; he hasn't the legs for it!'

'What do you mean?' roared the outraged soldier. 'I was chosen for my legs.'

'Yes,' laughed the little one, 'but *who* chose you, Queen Victoria?'

'You gotta admit it, soldier, your legs have seen better days,' croaked the leading cleaner.

'Yus,' said a slow one slowly, 'they have

gone bandy.'

'Bandy!' roared the Beefeater. 'My legs are *not* bandy!'

'Yes they are,' croaked the leader of the cleaning ladies. 'Now just move them a moment while I put the vacuum cleaner on.' She hauled a vast industrial vacuum cleaner into the room and began searching for a plug.

'It ain't just *his* legs what are bandy,' muttered the huge one, 'they've *all* got bandy legs!'

'No,' said the slow one, 'some of 'em are knock-kneed.'

'And look at the bright red noses on 'em,' croaked their leader. 'Call yourselves Queen's guards, I only hope she never has to look at you – the fright could kill her! Go on, move out the way!'

'There's nothing wrong with our noses,' snapped the Beefeater angrily.

'No – very good noses for seeing in the dark with!' cackled the little cleaner wickedly. 'I wish I had a nose like yours; I'd save a fortune on heating. The whole family could sit round it toasting muffins!'

It is always unwise to tease a Beefeater about his nose. Beefeaters remain calm at all other times, even when they are lopping off heads, but, where their noses are concerned, beefeaters are touchy. With a bloodcurdling cry the insulted soldier lifted his axe and bounded at them. Batty would have been hacked if he hadn't tripped over the huge hoover and crashed to the floor. Screaming and squawking the frightened ladies fled, leaving their brooms and dusters behind them.

Fortunately guards are not allowed to leave their posts even to go to the loo, so the outraged Beefeater contented himself by kicking the huge hoover until his toes hurt.

Dusk arrived and the ruthless ravens rattled their wings restlessly. Then, all at once, they wheeled round the stronghold like a swarm of evil spirits before flying off to the battlements where they roost by night.

Imagine trying to steal that treasure. First you'd have to climb up the high castle walls; then you'd have to sneak past the red-nosed soldiers; next you'd have to open the door – which is bolted from the inside; then you would have to fight your way to the Jewels while Beefeaters lopped bits off you. Finally your head would be taken out and stuck on a special spike on the battlements for the ravens to peck your eyes out.

That is the security system at the Tower of London. As you see, it leaves nothing to chance.

Now let me ask you a simple question: how would you like to have a go at pinching the Crown Jewels?

I see.

You would not like to have your eyes pecked out for breakfast. I don't blame you. But little Caroline

70

Crisp was *already hidden* in that closely guarded tower. Yes – she was waiting there bravely with one aim in her brain – to nick the lot!

You've guessed where she was hidden, haven't you?

Chapter 12

Exactly.

Caroline was lying comfortably in the Slurp Machine waiting until the soldiers were half asleep. The Slurp Machine was the name they'd given to the pretend vacuum cleaner that Nick had invented for stealing back Granny Fang's loot. It had a tiny periscope so that Caroline could look about from inside. The first thing she saw was the back of the Chief Beefeater's head; he had his back to the Slurp Machine of course, which made things easier. Cautiously Caroline slid her hand out of a trap door towards the largest, most glittering crown; carefully she lifted it up, and drew it into the machine; noiselessly she pushed it down into the swag sack which nestled at her feet. All through the long night Caroline's little hand reached out and grabbed:

crowns,
sceptres,
orbs,
and sacks of gold.

'This will teach the Granny Fang Gang,' smiled the Third Year girl. 'When they try to steal the Queen's treasure – it won't be there!'

How pleased the real Queen would be when she was told that the Fearless Four had saved her crown.

Caroline would almost certainly be made a Dame for her part in this adventure. Everyone would have to be respectful, even teachers like Sherbet Lemon. 'Dame Caroline,' he'd have to say, 'I am terribly sorry to have to tell you that all your sums were wrong but we are so honoured to have you at our school that you will still receive a credit' – that's the sort of thing that would happen. So the fearless, deeply-freckled girl dreamed the night away until the cleaning ladies came knocking at the door.

'You've got our vacuum cleaner in there, my lads,' croaked a voice. 'We need it to clean up. Open the door and shove it out for us!'

'Okay.'

It was about half an hour after the cleaning ladies had called that a trusty new squad of Beefeaters marched up to the stronghold and knocked thrice at the ancient door knocker.

'Who goes there?' cried the Chief haughtily.

'The Queen's Yeomen!' boomed a Beefeater from outside.

'What is the pass poem?' asked the Chief.

The Beefeaters replied together with a sing-song chorus:

> 'We're the Yeomen of England
> So dapper and smart;
> We don't have diseases,
> We're fit in each part.

73

We're awesome to look at –
So handsome and brave,
Born to fight fiercely
On land and on wave.

Our hair's free from dandruff,
Our underwear's clean,
Our teeth when we snarl at you
Glisten and gleam.

Our noses are luminous,
Our legs straight and true;
We are honest and fearless
And tougher than YOU!

We have emptied our potties
And made up our beds
And now we are ready
For lopping off heads!

That was the right answer; the bolts were pulled
back and the heavy door creaked open.

'The Jewels!' cried the first Beefeater to step into
the stronghold. 'They are gone!'

Chapter 13

'I am afraid Mr Lennon is ill,' announced the Thrasher, 'so I will be taking you on your outing.' The Third Years received this news coolly. They all believed that on a school trip to the Tower of London they would be much better off without Miss Thrasher.

'I hope she's not in one of her strops,' whispered Wayne Drain as he clambered into the coach.

'Yeh,' blinked Craig. He hadn't been expecting to be going on this trip; he'd thought it was next week, so he'd come without a packed lunch. Life is tough for vague people.

'Settle down, children,' yelled Miss Thrasher. 'If anyone feels sick please call for the bucket in good time. Anyone who's sick over another child will receive a black mark, is that clearly understood?'

'What if we're sick over a grown-up?' asked Sharon Slurrey.

'Two black marks!'

'That's not fair, Miss, it should be the same...'

'No – it thould be the other way wound,' protested Lucasta Smirk, 'becoth gwown upths are bigger, tho they're harder to mith!'

'Be quiet, Lucasta. Sit down everyone and read your notes. Remember you are doing projects about

75

knights and armour. Craig, what did we tell you yesterday about packed lunches?'

Craig looked blank. He'd forgotten when yesterday was. 'Miss Thrasher, Craig can have bits of other people's dinners,' suggested Wayne helpfully. 'We could pass the sick bucket down the coach and people could donate crisps and bits of cake and stuff – and Craig could eat it, Miss, for his packed lunch.'

'That is a very thoughtful idea, Wayne,' agreed the teacher.

That is how Craig ate a most nourishing meal which consisted of: one Smartie; two crisps; one apple core; seven crusts; one squashed grape; and the egg from an egg sandwich. What a lucky little chap!

When the coach arrived, Miss Thrasher led the Third Years over the drawbridge and stopped at the massive door of the mighty castle.

'It's shut!' cried Wayne – a most observant boy.

'That's not fair!' cried Lucasta Smirk. 'We've come thpecially.'

'Are they chopping someone's head off?' asked Sharon eagerly.

'Can we go and watch, Mith?'

'What's happening, Miss?'

'Ssh! Calm down, children. I will ring the bell.'

She stuck out a finger and jabbed.

'Gerroff!' roared an angry voice from the other side

of the door. The Thrasher had prodded the peephole and jabbed the Chief Beefeater in his eye.

'I'm sorry – I didn't realise it was someone's eye; I thought it was the doorbell.'

'We don't have doorbells; this is a castle not a bungalow. What do you want?'

'We want to look round.'

'Well you can't!' boomed the Chief Beefeater.

'But you're supposed to be open every day,' protested the Head.

'Well today we're not.'

'But I have brought these children a long way – we want to see the Crown Jewels.'

The Beefeater groaned; this was a very sore point – like his eye. 'Haven't you heard?' he asked. 'They've been pinched!'

The Third Years gaped. They were *dumbstruck*.

'Someone nicked 'em last night,' continued the Yeoman bitterly.

It was Lucasta Smirk's special wheedling face and her deeply simpering voice that got them into the Tower. Without her they'd have had to go home without seeing anything.

'Oh Mr Beefeater, pleath let uth in,' she simpered wheedlingly. 'We are only lickle childwin and we pwomith to be good.'

The sturdy Yeoman weakened; a lump stuck in his throat like a muffin.

'What's the point?' he replied mournfully. 'The

Crown Jewels are gone.'

'But we can thee the thoots of armour and the thords and daggers and the clubs and maces and the thpears and axes and the arrows and the ghosts of all the murdered people and the wavens pecking the eyes out of the thevered headth – lickle children like thingth like that!'

'All right then,' relented the Chief, 'but you will have to be escorted by me to make sure you don't get in the way of the police. Understand?'

'Yeth, Thir, thank you tho much. We will be ath good ath gold.'

The mighty door creaked open; Miss Thrasher and the Littlesprats entered the ancient castle. The Third Years were eerily silent as they trooped across the cobblestones led by the Chief Beefeater. Even chatterboxes like Sharon Slurrey were mute and dumb when they passed the blood-stained block where heads were hacked. They could feel waves of rage radiating from all the Beefeaters; you could tell that they were itching to chop a few heads off just to make themselves feel better. And all the while with whirring wings a cloud of ravens hovered overhead like vampires. 'Up here,' said the Chief Beefeater, turning up some steps and leading them into a long gallery full of suits of armour.

'This is the armour of Prince Peter the Peaceful,' he explained pointing at a suit of armour seated comfortably in an armchair. 'As you see, it is hardly

79

used. But this armour here – that's all dented and bashed about – was worn by King Richard Longsnozzel who fought in the War of the Noses.'

'Did he win?' asked Wayne.

'No. As you can see by the state of his armour, he came second.'

'It'th got a funny thmell,' complained Lucasta, 'ith he thtill inthide it?'

'Of course not!' frowned the Chief. But the little Smirk was quite right; there was an evil stench – as if someone with festering feet and ozone-friendly armpits was inside it. No wonder there'd been a War of the Noses.

Fortunately the Beefeater had moved on and was now standing in front of a dinky suit of armour.

'Who was that for?' asked Craig. 'Was it for a boy?'

'Yes,' replied the Yeoman solemnly, 'that is the armour of poor little King Edward the Unfortunate.'

'Wath he in the War of the Noses?'

'No,' replied the Beefeater sadly. 'He was one of the little princes in the Tower that were smothered. I'll show you the room where it happened in a minute.'

'I suppose they were being guarded by Beefeaters when they were done in,' whispered Wayne in one of those loud whispers that everyone is supposed to hear. The Chief Beefeater sighed and led the Third Years out of the armour gallery towards the tower in which the little princes had been smothered.

But one Third Year boy remained behind; he gazed entranced at the little suit of armour; he imagined putting it on, sitting on a charger and charging about.

'Craig! What are you doing?' whispered Wayne, who'd sneaked back to see where his friend had got to.

'I'm just looking at this boy's suit of armour,' explained Craig. 'I wonder if it's easy to get into.'

He clambered over the rope that kept the public back and touched the boy king's armour cautiously. But the boy king didn't seem too keen on being gawped at. His helmet suddenly turned with a creak and looked straight into Craig's frightened face.

'Go away!' it hissed.

It was then that King Richard Longsnozzel clanked to life; the huge, richly scented battle armour lurched towards the squealing boys.

Chapter 14

'And here are the little princes,' sniffed the Chief Beefeater dabbing his bloodshot eye with a Kleenex.

'I thought you said they'd been smothered,' complained Sharon. 'They look perfectly all right to me.'

'They were smothered,' explained the Beefeater. 'You don't think those are real boys, do you? Do you think we can just show people into the bedrooms of kings and queens when they're in 'em having a kip? Those aren't real princes; they're waxworks.'

The Third Years gazed critically at the waxwork princes.

'But they're breathing!' gasped Fatty Hardcastle.

'That's done by an electric motor,' explained the Chief.

'Are the thoots of armour worked by electric motors? Or are there ghosts inthide them?'

'What? Who said that?'

'Me – Lucathta Thmirk – I'm here by the window and I can thee thome thoots of armour wunning down the thteps of the tower we just came out of. Cwaig and Wayne are wunning in fwont of them! Look!'

'What's happening?' screamed all the Third Years

83

who couldn't get to look because of all the other Third Years clustering feverishly round the window.

'Lotth of Beefeaters!' squeaked Lucasta excitedly. 'Oh look! Wooks!'

'Ravens!' corrected the Chief Beefeater.

'Wavens then. How thimply thtunning. Now all the other Beefeaters are hacking at the thoots of armour – listen to the cwashing and the slashing! Oh look – it'th the detective that came to thee us at thchool. He looks very thmart – with a wose in his teeth – there's lots of other thmart young men and ladies with woses in their hair. They are dancing wound the ghosts and the Beefeaters.'

'It's the Metropolitan Police Dance Display Unit!' cried Miss Thrasher, who'd shoved her way to the front and could now see over Lucasta's head. 'They have rescued Wayne and Craig and, good gracious, they appear to be arresting one of the ghosts – a weeny one. But the ravens are attacking the Beefeaters – they seem to be confused. This is terrible. The other ghosts are escaping!'

'They got away, sir,' reported one of the policewomen. She'd lost the rose from her hair, her dress had been torn, her ears had been pecked and she was angry.

'Never mind!' chuckled the dancing detective. 'Let's see what's in this sack.' He ripped a sack from the iron hands of the small suit of armour standing beside him. 'What have we here? The Queen's crown and sceptre! Well, well, well!'

'But...'

'Shut your evil little trap! Let's see who you are...I should have guessed – Caroline Crisp! You were never kidnapped at all, were you? You've been out robbing all the time, haven't you?'

'Fanthy Cawoline being a wobber!'

'Yeh – and stealing the Crown Jewels!'

'An' all the time we thought she'd been kid-napped!'

The bus buzzed with talk like that all the way back to Littlesprat.

'Are you going to be thick, Mith Fwasher? Do you want the thick bucket?'

'No, Lucasta, thank you very much.'

'But you look very pale, Mith, as if you felt thick.'

'Go back to your seat, child, and take the bucket with you.'

'Yeth, Mith.'

But the Thrasher did look sick and she felt sick – as sick as a parrot with foul pest. 'It's not fair,' she grumbled to herself. 'To think, I walked right past those suits of armour and didn't spot a thing... I will be a laughing stock – an amateur detective who just stood about looking puzzled while the police nabbed a baddie for the crime of the century.'

Miss Thrasher was still in a miffed mood next day. Every time she heard a child laugh she screamed at it because she thought the whole school was laughing at her for being a defective detective. And, of course, she was right. The whole school was laughing at her – apart from Sherbet Lemon who was too sweet to laugh at other people's misfortunes.

TAP

TAP

TAP

There was a nervous tap at the Thrasher's door during break on the morning after Caroline's arrest.

'Come in.'

The Lemon bounced into her office and stood stammering.

'Well, Herbert, what is it?'

'It's about Caroline Crisp, Miss Thrasher, do you think she really stole the Crown Jewels?'

'Yes. Of course she did. We all saw – she had a lot of them in her sack. She and the other members of her gang, the ones that escaped, must be very cunning criminals indeed. It was pure luck that prancing fool arrested her, but, of course, he'll make out he'd been on Caroline's trail all the time and tracked her down by his detective skills.'

'But,' squeaked Sherbet, 'on TV the police always arrest the wrong people and amateur detectives go sleuthing round and discover the truth. And the innocent person the police arrest always looks terribly guilty with piles of evidence against them. Maybe that's what's happened to Caroline.'

The Thrasher perked up. 'That's absolutely true, Herbert, Perry Mason's whole life is dedicated to getting people off murder charges when the police have arrested them by mistake.'

'You could do the same for Caroline.'

'Perhaps I could,' agreed the Thrasher. 'I could take a couple of weeks off school in order to teach Caroline, then no one would twig what I was really up to.'

'Teach her?'

'Yes, she has to be educated even though she's a criminal. I will volunteer to do it.'

'But who'd be Head here?'

'Well, not you – that's for certain. Or any of the other teachers here – I'm not having any of my staff getting above themselves. I shall advertise for a relief headteacher and take on the Caroline Crisp case.'

'I hope you manage to prove she's innocent.'

'Yes. If I did, she wouldn't have to have her head chopped off!'

Chapter 15

'Thank Gawd we don't 'ave to talk posh no more!' croaked Granny Fang.

'Nor sleep in them 'orrible tents,' grunted Sludge.

'It was fun camping out under the stars,' chuckled little Batty. 'I specially liked the sing-songs round the fire and pretending to be Nick – saying things like, "I say how ripping!" – it was great!'

'It was all right for you,' grumbled Sludge, 'but it weren't no fun being a girl called Horace and it was really hard for Slow – wasn't it, dear?'

Slow blinked blankly.

'It was hard for you pretending to be Gwendolin', wasn't it?'

'Yes. I am Gwendolin'. I *hate* spiders.'

'You don't have to be Gwendolin' no more,' cackled Batty. 'You can go back to being your old self.'

'What old self?' asked Slow. She'd forgotten she was really Slow – this was because she was really slow. Understand?

'Remember your real name? Slow. Say it – say your real name.'

'Your real name.'

'Never mind, dear,' laughed Batty, 'you was wonderful as Gwendolin' and don't she look lovely with that crown on 'er 'ead?'

All the dinner ladies were wearing crowns; and they all dripped with glitter; they had got most of the Queen's treasure, you see, only the stuff that had been in Caroline's sack had been recovered by the Dance Display Unit.

'It's a pity Caroline got nicked,' sighed Batty.

'No it's not,' grunted Sludge. 'I'm glad that little sap's for the chop.'

'Yeh,' agreed Slow, 'it serves 'er right. It was because of 'er I had to wear that dress and talk posh.'

'But what if she grasses on us?' growled Sludge with a frown. 'She might point the finger at us – tell the cops what we done!'

'But she thinks we was the Fearless Four,' Batty pointed out. 'She don't know we had anything to do with it. Besides, she thinks the police are baddies – so I don't expect she'll say anything to them at all. She'll just sit tight in prison and wait for the Fearless Four to rescue her!'

'She'll have a long wait then,' laughed Sludge.

'She might talk,' growled Granny. 'She knows it was Batty and me that kidnapped her in the first place and if she says anything about the Fearless Four, then the cops might put two and two together and come looking for us!'

'We'll have to hide,' agreed Sludge.

'Yeh – lie low,' nodded Granny.

'How?' asked Slow.

'Same as usual...' cackled Batty.

'Not...not pretending to be dinner ladies,' grumbled Mrs Sludge.

'Why not?' asked Batty. 'It's always worked in the past. Whenever we've had to lie low we've just signed on as dinner ladies and waited for the fuss to die down. Being dinner ladies is by far the best disguise because all dinner ladies are rough and tough like us, so we just blend in.'

'I know, but couldn't we do something else for a change? Something where we wouldn't have to wash up or clean tables or cook all day long? There must be other jobs where we'd blend in...'

'Such as?' asked Granny.

'Well...'

'What sort of job could you find where people like us could just blend in?' Granny demanded to know. 'People like Batty what is a bit touched or you, Sludge, what is huge and savage or me who can be...hasty...or Slow – who's thick and evil?'

'We could be *teachers!*' cried Batty suddenly. 'We could blend in as teachers all right!'

'Yeh.'

'Yeh.'

'Dur!'

'That's a good suggestion, Batty,' said Granny Fang with a sharkish smile. 'And, as it happens, there's an advert for a Headteacher's job in the local

paper. It would suit me nicely. Listen to this...'

With a rustle of paper, Granny found the place
and read as follows: 'Temporary Headteacher re-
quired for Littlesprat County Primary School. Must
be strict.'

'You're strict,' yelped Batty.

'Yes,' chuckled Granny, 'I'll apply.'

'You might be strict,' said Sludge, 'but can you do
sums?'

'You don't have to be able to do sums to be
a teacher,' explained Batty. 'They've got all the
answers in a little book. They just pretend to be good
at sums!'

'Batty's right,' explained Granny. 'I'll apply for the job of Headteacher – we'll nobble the other candidates – and as soon as I'm in charge, I'll sack the other teachers and appoint you lot instead. Then all the coppers in England can hunt high and low – they'll never find us!'

Chapter 16

'But I don't see the point of learning how to do tricky sums if they're about to chop my head off,' protested Caroline. Miss Thrasher had been ushered into her dark cell in the damp dungeons of the Tower.

'What an extraordinary attitude,' cried the teacher, 'typical of the slack approach of the modern child!'

But Caroline Crisp was not interested in hearing Miss Thrasher's views on the modern child. 'It's not fair!' she cried. 'I haven't done anything bad!'

'But surely, Caroline, stealing the Crown Jewels was very naughty.' Miss Thrasher stopped talking for a moment because she noticed that Caroline's green eyes were blazing and she'd gone deeply pale. She stamped a fierce foot on the hard floor.

'What about you!' cried the angry child. 'You're the one that's really bad. Not me! I was trying to save the Crown Jewels from the Fang Gang – but you were working for them!'

'I beg your pardon?'

'You were one of their minders!'

'What?'

Caroline fought to control her temper. Eventually she replied – but her voice was squeaky. 'You know what I mean, Miss Thrasher, you minded money for them – you and Mr Lennon – I saw you counting it!'

'What? Where were you?'

'In the Slurp Machine. The others had pretended to be cleaners...'

'What others?' asked Miss Thrasher suspiciously, but Caroline ignored her and surged on squeakily. 'They left it in your office with me inside – so I know everything!'

'You poor child, your misfortunes have driven you mad. Work for Granny Fang – me? I'm good...'

'But Nick and Jasper said you were in the pay of Granny Fang – and I saw you counting great piles of money...'

Miss Thrasher waited for a second or so before replying. She fixed Caroline with a rattlesnake stare, took a deep breath, tilted up her nose until it was at its most impressively snooty angle, and breathed out again with an enormous sigh.

'Good gracious, girl, you don't seriously believe that I am a criminal, do you? You are the one that has been rushing about with this Nick and Jasper pinching stuff. Who are these people anyway?'

'They are the boys in the Fearless Four,' cried Caroline defiantly. 'And we were *not* stealing stuff; we were re-stealing it – getting it back from the people that were minding it. People like you!'

'You absurd child. Even if you are capable of believing that I was working for those terrible Dinner

95

Ladies, surely you couldn't believe the same of Mr Lennon – who wouldn't hurt a fly.'

'Yes, but...'

'Besides,' continued the Thrasher curtly, 'criminals don't ask other people to mind their money for them – it'd be too dangerous. The minders would pinch it for themselves, wouldn't they?'

'Yes, but...'

'And anyway, who are the Fearless Four?'

'They are like the Famous Five. They're detectives and they go about having adventures and eating ham sandwiches and having fun...'

'And they said I was a criminal, did they?'

'Yes.'

'And you believed them?'

'Yes. I...'

'And you took that money from my room?'

'Yes, because...'

'Was it you that stole the cups from the Police Dance Display Unit?'

'Yes. They're criminals too.'

'No they're not. Stupid – yes. Criminals – no. Caroline, you have been tricked!'

'But...'

'Was it the so-called Fearless Four that persuaded you to steal the Crown Jewels?'

'No. It was the other way round. You see one of the Dinner Ladies, Batty, is going about disguised as the Queen – part of a con-trick to get hold of the

Crown Jewels, so I thought if we could hide them then ...'

'Hush, girl, ssh! Start at the beginning. Tell me everything that happened starting with the nit nurses.'

'Yes, Miss Thrasher, these two nit nurses came in through the window and ...' The unhappy child blurted out her simple story.

When she'd finished, Miss Thrasher remained silent. Caroline lay down in the straw and waited. At length the Thrasher spoke. 'It all seems quite clear,' she said.

'Does it, Miss?'

'Yes. Remember, Caroline, that I have read all the Miss Marple books. I am as keen on them as you are on the Famous Five. Reading Miss Marple books has given me an insight into the criminal mind.'

But Caroline never heard Miss Thrasher's explanation for, with a rattle of keys, the door creaked open. A beefy voice spoke in the deep, damp gloom: 'Caroline Crisp – it's time.'

'Time for what?'

'For the chop,' answered the Chief Beefeater calmly.

'This is disgraceful,' yelled Miss Thrasher. 'This child is innocent! Her zeal for doing good has been fiendishly twisted by cunning villains. Besides, she is a pupil of Littlesprat Primary School!'

'So what?'

'You can't go about recklessly chopping the heads off children from Littlesprat. The Headteacher is paid according to the number of children's heads in the school! If you cut one of them off, the Head's salary will be cut too!'

'I can't help that,' replied the Beefeater with a sigh. 'People caught nicking the Crown Jewels get their heads chopped of – that's the law.'

'But the child was tricked. I insist that the execution is stopped. I have important new evidence...'

'That's what they all say. Come on, Caroline, I have to ... to take you to ... *sniff* the block ... and ... and ...' A tear rolled down his manly cheek.

'But I have given up some of my valuable time to teach this girl sums!'

'Bit late for that,' sobbed the Chief. 'Don't blame us Beefeaters,' he managed to gulp as he led the worried child out of her cell. 'We all refused to chop your little, freckled head off.' He blew his nose with an ancient paper hanky. 'It was only when they offered to pay us double that we agreed, so don't judge us too hard, my dear.'

Caroline wanted to say something brave and funny, but her brain was blank and her tongue was frozen, so she didn't.

Even Miss Thrasher was silent; she followed behind clutching her book of sums. Maybe if there was time she'd be able to explain about fractions. The

Chief led them out into the sunlight. The courtyard was thronged with weeping Beefeaters; were any of them Nick and Jasper in disguise, Caroline wondered. Ravens rustled their black wings hungrily.

'Kneel down,' said a muffled voice. It was muffled because it belonged to the executioner who wore a hood over his head – maybe that was Jasper!

'Just rest your neck on it,' said the muffled voice.

'Such a shame,' blubbed a Beefeater.

'So young,' cried another.

'Still, she'll know another time,' reflected the Chief.

How true.

The block was a bit sticky, but Caroline didn't notice. Out of the corner of an eye she saw the heavy axe rise. Quickly she shut her eyes. Tight. Were Nick and Jasper there? Would they save her?

What do you think?

Chapter 17

Caroline's eyes were tight shut but she could hear and smell. The block smelt like a butcher's shop and the ravens were cawing hungrily. 'Nick and Jasper aren't here,' she told herself quickly. You have to think quickly when your head is on the block otherwise a thought might not get finished in time.

Another quick thought whizzed through the girl's red head: 'But I'm sure they tried their very, very best,' she thought – just in time.

WHOOSH!

Caroline felt herself shoot up into the air. 'Gosh!' she thought. 'I'm going up to heaven!'

It's a bit worrying when you discover you're a spirit. Particularly when an angel screams at you as you're whizzing up to heaven with your ghostly eyes shut tight.

'Are you all right?' bellowed the angel.

'Of course I'm not,' yelped the girl. 'I've just been executed!'

'No you haven't; I rescued you!'

Caroline opened her eyes. Miss Thrasher's upside-down face was peering at her; she held tight round Caroline's ankles and yelled down at her. 'These are the pants of power – my new invention!'

But Caroline was not looking at the balloon pants; she glanced at London spread far below and shut her green eyes again. Her ankles slipped a little despite the Thrasher's fierce fingers.

'We'll soon be down again,' yelled the amateur detective. 'The gas seeps out slowly and we will gradually descend and land. Luckily there's a bit of a breeze which'll waft us a long way from the Tower.'

When Caroline opened her eyes again the ground was coming up to meet them. It was like descending very fast in a lift without a floor. They hit the ground with a thump – if it had been a road or a roof or a pavement Caroline might have broken a leg. But it was not a road or a roof, it was grass.

'We're in some sort of park,' cried Miss Thrasher as she wrestled with the belt of the pants of power which had gone saggy and crinkled.

'Look at all those dogs,' said Caroline anxiously.

'Dogs!' yelled the teacher. 'Those aren't dogs! They're wolves; we've landed in the zoo!'

Chapter 18

WHOOSH!!

Whenever Miss Thrasher pulled a rip cord the feeling in Caroline's tummy was one thousand times worse than what tummies feel like on a big-dipper. They shot up into the sky until the watching wolves could only see a speck.

Have you ever been to a fête and bought one of those balloons which you send up off into the sky? Have you ever stood watching your balloon get weenier and teenier while you hoped it would be blown all the way to France so that you'd win the big prize? Well, a moment comes when you can't see the speck any more; you search and stare keenly with a hand maybe shielding your eyes from the sun. But your balloon's gone. Is it going onward and upward? Is it shrivelling and falling? You can't see. Well, that's what it was like for the wolves, except they didn't shield their eyes from the sun with their paws. Being wolves they just gazed amazed at the empty sky for a while and then loped wolfishly about extra fast and frisky because of the excitement. Red-headed girls with freckles suddenly crashing out of the sky is worrying for wolves; it gets them agitated.

It also agitates policemen and policewomen; at least the Metropolitan Police Dance Display Unit was deeply disturbed when Caroline and Miss Thrasher landed on them while they were doing a house-to-house conga.

Ever since the nimble team of dancing crimebusters had arrested Caroline they had been full of zip and pep. It's true they hadn't nabbed the whole gang and that most of the Queen's crowns were still missing, but catching Caroline had been smart. Now the Dance Unit was known all over planet Earth as an ace crimebusting outfit. Ordinary policemen – with big feet – who'd been laughing and scoffing when the Dance Cups had been nicked, were now full of respect.

So the dapper detective and his team went about with bounce, flounce and extra pep. You could tell that just by watching them conducting a house-to-house search for the rest of the crowns. The Chief rang bells and, as doors were opened, he led the talented team inside each house. From room to room they danced in lively line, each gallant copper clutching tightly round the waist of the dainty lady cop in front of him. When every room had been pranced through, the Chief led the dancers out again while the tuneful team sang gustily:

> 'The Police Formation Conga
> Can stay with you no longa
> We're calling door to door-a
> And have to do some more-a...'

It was heartlifting to see these happy heroes lurching tunefully from house to house...

'We're searching for some baddies
And for where their swag is...'

And the brightest, zippiest cop of the lot was their sprightly leader, his black hair glistening, his brown eyes gleaming and his nimble feet twinkling...

'Police Formation Conga
Stay with you no longa
Call in door to door-a
Longlegs of the law-a...'

Even muggers and snatchers cheered – especially when a flying girl drifted down the street and hovered for a second over the Chief's head.

'What are you doing up there?' yelled the dapper one.

'Nothing,' replied the girl. 'I'm just hanging about. I'm not doing anything wrong. I...'

'Look!' screamed an observant policewoman springing out of the conga. 'It's Caroline Crisp!' She chased down the road, leapt up, grabbed at the flying child – but missed.

'After them!' yelled the detective.

Chapter 19

Who would have thought that Slow would have turned out to be an ace teacher? 'One and one is eleven,' she explained patiently to the eager little First Year Juniors that she had in her class. Granny Fang had the job of temporary head of Little-sprat, you see, and immediately sacked the real teachers – like dear Sherbet – and appointed Batty, Sludge and Slow instead. They all wore the most stunning disguises with old-fashioned gowns and mortar boards. A mortar board looks like this:

And when Granny Fang's all girl gang were wearing them they looked like this:

Mrs Bang

Miss Batter

Mrs Trudge   Mrs Thump

As you see, they look most learned and respectable. And Slow was the most learned of all and especially good at teaching sums. She was the one that was pretending to be called Mrs Thump and, on the afternoon Caroline was to be executed, she gave the eager little First Years an extra-long lesson on sums as a special treat.

'One three is three,' her slow voice chanted tunefully. 'Two threes are thirty-three, three threes are ... er ... dur ... '

'Please, Mrs Thump, our teacher said two threes were six,' gulped a little First Year nervously.

'What,' replied Slow, 'your old teacher said two trees were sick, did she?'

'No, she said two threes were six!'

'That's daft,' explained the new teacher wisely. She picked up her pink chalk and slowly wrote two threes on the blackboard.

'See?' she said. 'That's two threes, isn't it – there's one and there's the other one – two threes, right?'

'Yes, Mrs Thump,' chorused the First Years.

'Well I can't see no six there – can you?'

'No, Mrs Thump,' replied the chorus.

'What can you see?'

'Two threes,' sang half the class.

'Thirty-three,' sang the other.

'Exactly,' nodded their new teacher wisely. 'You don't want to bother about nothing your old teacher said. She was daft, wasn't she?'

'Yes, Mrs Thump,' sang the chorus.

'That is why she was sacked,' continued Mrs Thump. 'Wasn't it?'

'Yes, Mrs Thump,' agreed the First Years.

It was nice having a really good teacher who had the knack of explaining sums so that they seemed easy.

In the next classroom the Second Years were learning how to bet on horses; Mrs Trudge had just gone round collecting their money and turned the television on ready for the three o'clock race from Newmarket.

'There they are,' she said pointing at the screen,

'going round the paddock. Now listen carefully to what the man says so you can identify the horse you have backed. Remember – if your horse wins you win some of this money and how much you win is worked out according to the odds, okay? So if your horse is 100 to one then you get a pound for every penny you bet, understand?'

'Cor!'

'Yeh!'

'Remember it's important that the modern child learns to work out odds correctly. Your old teacher neglected this – which is one of the reasons she was sacked – so you've got a lot of catching up to do...'

'Yes, Mrs Trudge.'

The Fourth Year class was also having to work hard to catch up.

'Jason. What was that I just said?' croaked Mrs Bang.

'You said that winning at cards was not just a matter of luck, Mrs Bang.'

'No it ain't,' agreed the teacher. 'To win at cards you gotta be artful. You gotta cheat – but you gotta do it in a way that the punters you are playing with don't realise, see? And it is the same with dice, understand?'

'Yes, Mrs Bang.'

'Your old teacher shamefully neglected this side of

your education. I don't know what would have happened to you when you went to big school – you'd of been fleeced – specially if you'd played poker with the teachers. Never mind, my dears, with my intensive instruction you'll clean up! It'll be you that does the fleecing!'

'Cor!'

'Great!'

As you see, Granny Fang and her teaching team were doing really useful work. Particularly Batty, who had to deal with the Third Years on the day of the execution.

'Now, Third Years, I know that you're all sad about poor little Caroline,' cried Batty.

'Pleath, Mith Batter, hath it happened yet?'

Batty looked at her watch and sighed. 'She was due to be beheaded at two o'clock today,' she explained, 'and it is now three o'clock.'

There was silence.

'It's not often that a Third Year child is beheaded,' continued Batty brightly. 'In fact the last time it happened was in eleven hundred and forty three when Princess Rachael the Reckless had her head chopped off for sticking her tongue out at King Bonehead the Bonkers.'

'Woth he thad, Mith, after he had done it?'

'Yes, Lucasta, he was. It says in this book she came and haunted him with her head under her arm. That often happens when people have been be-

headed for no reason; they come back as ghosts to haunt the guilty ones...'

There was a single, horrified scream. Then everyone yelled. Batty wet herself with fright. A deeply freckled head was hovering outside the window.

'It'th Cawoline'th head, Mith; upside down, Mith; it must have come back, Mith, to haunt the guilty!'

Chapter 20

'Oh look at it!' wailed Batty, forgetting her Miss Batter voice. ''Er little freckled head hovering and wothering all by itself!'

'Oh my Gawd!' howled Granny Fang as she swept into the classroom to investigate the screaming.

'It – it's Caroline's ghost head,' explained Wayne hoarsely when the other two teachers came rushing in.

'Upside down,' said Craig – in case they hadn't noticed. 'The window's open; it might float inside!'

'You can thee wite up her nothe,' gurgled Lucasta, 'and look there'th the detective that awested her. I ecthpect Cawoline ith haunting him to therve him wight.'

The sprightly leader of the Metropolitan Police Ballroom Dance Display team was certainly outside the window. His dapper little napper turned this way and that – sometimes looking up at Caroline's ghost head and sometimes into the classroom.

'Hullo, ghost,' called Slow from inside. She liked spooky things. 'Remember me? I was ... er ... Gwendolin' when we was the Fearless Four. The rest of 'em are here too pretending to be teachers. Look, Batty has wet herself and Granny is kneeling down saying her prayers. But I like ghosts and creepy things. I got comics of them.'

'Go away – back where you came from. We're sorry for what we done!' wailed Batty's little voice.

Slow gazed at Caroline's head, entranced. 'Granny and Batty said you was green but you ain't green, are you? You got red hair and a little freckled face.'

'Don't do nothing evil to us,' croaked Granny's voice.

'We didn't mean no harm, my dear,'

'We are truly sorry for what we done,' wailed Batty.

'It was Granny and Batty that tricked you. It was their idea,' gibbered Sludge. 'So leave me alone. Just haunt them two!'

'Hullo,' blinked Slow. She'd suddenly remembered her manners and was greeting the dancing detective and the members of his clean and sprightly team that were clustering round the window.

'That's a ghost up there. Hovering it is. It's the ghost head of a little girl what has had her head chopped off. She was called Caroline. I knew her when she was alive, didn't I, Caroline?'

'Yes,' replied the ghost.

'See?' said Slow looking proudly at the detective and his talented team. They seemed very interested in all she had to say.

'We got the Queen's stuff stacked in the headteacher's office all in sacks. It's a pity you are upside down or I could of given you a crown to wear. I like wearing the big crown best.'

'I expect you like bracelets too,' said the dapper detective kindly.

'Yeah, I do like bracelets.'

'Well I've got some heavy metal bracelets for you and your friends,' he told her.

Caroline was just thinking she'd stick her ghostly tongue out at Lucasta Smirk, when Miss Thrasher, hanging on to a drainpipe, let go of her legs and she fell into the waiting arms of the dancing detective.

As soon as he'd put her safely on the ground, the dapper one bounded gracefully through the class-room window while, at exactly the right moment, the disco-dancing martial arts coppers hurled open the classroom door.

'Right,' laughed the detective. 'Here are your heavy metal bracelets!'

The wondering Third Years gaped as Mrs Bang and the rest of the teachers were handcuffed. 'Chain 'em together,' ordered the detective, 'and get 'em down to the station. It looks as if hours of thought and hard work have paid off – we've nabbed the Crown Jewel gang.'

'I beg your pardon,' snapped an icy voice. Miss Thrasher had managed to wriggled out of the pants of power and had come striding into the room in her knickers.

'Stop sniggering!' she roared. 'What do you mean

you have nabbed them? You arrested Caroline, a perfectly innocent Third Year girl. It was me that rescued her. And it was due entirely to my cunning that the Dinner Lady Gang confessed! Caroline! What are you doing outside the window? Come in at once and sit in your place. We will continue with a few hard sums!'

Chapter 21

Slow was happy.

'Heavy metal bracelets are my favourite,' she gurgled jangling hers.

'Stop it,' growled Granny.

'Why?'

''Cos you're chained to Sludge, aren't you?'

'Yeh.'

'And Sludge is chained to Batty, ain't she?'

'Yuh.'

'And Batty is chained to me. Understand? So when you clank – we all clank. Just play with yer balloon and shut up.'

They were still in the playground under the watchful guard of the Display team. Soon the police van would arrive to take them to the Tower. You know what'll happen there, don't you?

Exactly.

No wonder Granny looked grim. No wonder Sludge was nearly fainting. No wonder Batty was looking madly about for a way of escape.

'Stop them balloon pants from bouncing on my head,' grumbled Sludge. 'Just let go and let them fly off.'

'No. They're mine. I like 'em. I got 'em tied to my chain. See?'

Batty glanced up at the pants. They were even more crinkled and wrinkled by now and wafted feebly over Slow's happy head. A cord bobbed down from the patent pants. *Emergency — Pull Cord* said a label.

'Well, this is an emergency,' thought Batty to herself. 'I'll give it a go!' She stretched up a hand and gave it a yank:

WHOOSH!

Another Knight Book

Allan Rune Pettersson

FRANKENSTEIN'S AUNT

'Next stop Frankenstein!' Aunt Frankenstein
has arrived determined to restore her
nephew's devastated castle to order and clear
the family's blackened name! An hilariously
spooky sequel to the famous Frankenstein
story.

Another Knight Book

John Antrobus

HELP! I AM A PRISONER IN A TOOTHPASTE FACTORY

As Ronnie is cleaning his teeth one morning, he sees a message written in the toothpaste: 'HELP!' it reads, 'I AM A PRISONER IN A TOOTHPASTE FACTORY!' Later there is an even more urgent appeal: 'HELP! THERE'S NOT MUCH TIME!'

So, with the somewhat dubious help of Uncle Roger, Ronnie sets off on the toothpaste trail, desperately trying to avoid the wicked clutches of the chemist. But when Mum and Dad are imprisoned in Glum's Toothpaste Factory, Ronnie's mission becomes even more dangerous. Can he solve the whole extraordinary mystery before he, too, becomes a prisoner?

Also in the same series:

THE BOY WITH ILLUMINATED MEASLES
RONNIE AND THE GREAT KNITTED ROBBERY

David Tinkler

THE HEADMASTER WENT SPLAT!

A Twerp Mystery

'Kevin Twerp,' hissed Killer Keast, the
ferocious headmaster of Shambles School, 'I
want to see you in my room immediately.'

Suddenly, it seemed to go cold. The light
went dim. There was a gasp from the children
and the teachers shivered. Kevin felt faint
and his mouth went dry.

Kevin Twerp's life hasn't been easy;
pop-singing dad killed in an air crash, Mum –
Nitty Norah the Hair Explorer – driven out to
work as a school nurse. And, looming, like a
dark shadow, Killer Keast.

But, with the help of WPC Rose Button,
lodger and All-England Mud Wallowing
Champion, things *will* change . . .!

Another Knight Book

David Tinkler

THE CASE OF THE FEEBLE WEEBLE

Think about your own dear school. Is it
shabby and in need of a lick of paint? Are the
teachers a bane and a pain?

Well Shambles School is EVEN WORSE!
However mad and bad your teacher may be,
he or she is meek and mild compared with
Killer Keast.

From the author of *The Headmaster Went Splat*
this is another outrageous school detective
story featuring the extraordinary Twerp
family, Policewoman Rose Button and, of
course, Killer Keast, the most feared
Headmaster in the universe.

Another Knight Book

David Tinkler

THE SCOURGE OF THE DINNER LADIES

CHOMP   CHOMP   BURP   SLURP
This was the noise of dinner time. Nobody
dared to talk.

'Who was that?' yelled Mrs Sludge.
'WHO WAS WHISPERING?'

There were some tough new dinner ladies at
Littlesprat Primary School: The Granny
Fang Gang. Mrs Sludge was the roughest,
toughest dinner lady that there has ever been.
And now she was brandishing her ladle!

Could the pupils of Littlesprat survive The
Scourge of the Dinner Ladies?